Book No. 6

Gladys the Dragon and The Mountain Bike

Written by
Elsie Bell

Illustrated by
Ray Schofield

Gladys the Dragon Series
edited by
Roger Wickham

Pond View Books

About these stories

Gladys is a sleepy, friendly dragon who doesn't fly any more. She will tell you she has 'quite given it up'. But in her dreams she **does** fly and, in this adventure, she flies off again to a castle of long ago to see Lady Gwendolyn. Gladys also wears her special T-shirt again. Do you remember how she got it in 'Gladys Saves the Day'?

The dragon's best friend is George, an eight year old boy who lives near the farm where Gladys has made her home in a small cave on a rocky hillside.

In the last book, Gladys met Lady Gwendolyn for the first time whilst George was drawing a castle for a competition. This book continues that story.

Gladys has many more adventures.

I hope you enjoy them all.

Elsie Bell.

This is where Gladys and George live.

The Mountain Bike

George was very, **very** excited.

In the last story, George was sending off his picture of a castle to a magazine art competition. Do you remember how Gladys helped him?

Well, it must have been a good picture, because he had received a letter from the editor of the magazine who congratulated him and said that he had won first prize for his excellent drawing. There had been hundreds of entries from all over the country but his was the best one.

The letter said that his prize would be delivered on Thursday of the next week. Well, that week was the l-o-n-g-e-s-t week of George's life, and his parents' life too, probably!

Every day, he would say to his mum or dad, "Is it Thursday today, Mum?" or, "Is it Thursday today, Dad?"

George had a letter from the editor.

Finally, on Wednesday, he asked the same question, "Is it Thursday today, Dad?"

"It's Thursday **tomorrow**, George," said Dad.

That night, when he was tucked up in bed, George said to his dad, "It really, really **is** Thursday tomorrow, isn't it Dad?"

"Yes George, it really, really is, **now go to sleep**." Some hope, his dad might just as well have told him to fly to the moon.

Morning came, eventually, and a few hours later, his prize was delivered to his home by a jolly man in a lorry. George tore off all the padded wrapping as fast as he could. And there it was. A really cool, very shiny, super duper, top-of-the-range mountain bike. Something he had always wanted.

He couldn't wait to show Gladys his new bike. "Come on boy, walkies," said George to his little dog Kerry, who was having great fun tearing up all the packaging that the bike had been wrapped in.

George unwraps his new mountain bike.

Poor little Kerry, it was more like **runnies** than **walkies**, trying to keep up with George on his new bike.

The dragon had just wandered out of her cave when she saw George riding along the track across the field towards her, calling, **"Gladys, Gladys, look at my new bike."**

When he got closer, he said, "Look Gladys, a mountain bike, it's my prize for that drawing of a castle that you helped me with."

Gladys got quite giddy watching George ride backwards and forwards in front of her. He was far too excited to get off the bike, and kept calling out, **"Guess how many gears it's got?"**

But he was always away again before Gladys could answer.

At last, after riding up and down about twenty times, George jumped off the bike and brought it to show Gladys all the different gears and bits and pieces.

George rode across the field to Gladys.

"It's got 21 gears, Gladys, **twenty one gears**."

"Mmm, a mountain bike with twenty one gears," repeated Gladys. You could tell she was impressed.

George pointed out every little detail until, at last, Gladys found herself gently nodding off to sleep. She started to have one of her regular dreams about a castle that looked very much like the one that George had drawn for the art competition.

In her dreams Gladys could fly, and in those days of long ago her wings always seemed bigger and stronger than they were now.

As she approached the castle, she could see Lady Gwendolyn standing on the battlements, jumping up and down and waving excitedly.

Lady Gwendolyn saw Gladys getting nearer and nearer, until she landed with a wibbly wobbly bump next to her.

Gladys saw Lady Gwendolyn waving.

She gave Gladys a great big hug. She was so pleased to see her friendly dragon again. Life in the castle was often quite boring, having to do needlework she didn't like.

"Can I have a ride please?" said Lady Gwendolyn.

She had started to climb on Gladys's back while she was hugging her, and the dragon thought that a ride was a splendid idea.

Off they went, circling the turrets of the castle before flying away over the forest. And then, in her dream, Gladys and Lady Gwendolyn landed together in the field beside George's beautiful new mountain bike.

Lady Gwendolyn jumped off the dragon's back, but she was rather chilly after all that flying so Gladys did a few of her gentle r-r-rumbly breaths to warm her up again.

"Ooh, that was lovely, thank you Gladys," she said, as she walked round and round the bike looking very puzzled.

Gladys flew off with Lady Gwendolyn.

George came running into the field and looked just as puzzled to see a girl wearing such very old fashioned clothes.

Gladys introduced them.

"Lady Gwendolyn, this is my friend George. George, this is Lady Gwendolyn who lives in a castle like the one you drew for the competition. And this is Kerry."

"Woof, woof," said Kerry.

Lady Gwendolyn patted Kerry on the head. But she was astonished when, holding out her hand to George, he just shook it politely. She was used to people either kissing her hand or bowing to her, but of course George didn't know this.

"Can you tell me what this is, please?" said Lady Gwendolyn pointing to the bike.

"It's a mountain bike and it goes like the wind," said George, "and it's got **twenty one gears.**"

George shook her hand politely.

Then he jumped onto the bike and rode quickly down the track, laughing as he went faster and faster.

"Oh, that's marvellous, please may I have a ride?" asked Lady Gwendolyn.

The bike kept falling over as she tried to get on it, so George held it for her. She sat sideways on the saddle, which was very uncomfortable, and wondered what to do next.

"How do I make it go?" Lady Gwendolyn looked quite bewildered.

"You can't sit sideways like that," replied George, "but with that long skirt I don't think you will be able to ride it properly anyway."

Then he had a bright idea. He jumped on his bike again and rode off calling, **"Just wait there a few minutes. I won't be long."**

Lady Gwendolyn sat sideways on the bike.

He was wearing one of his favourite T-shirts with a big **G** on it, and was soon back with a spare one and a pair of jeans.

By then Gladys had put on **her** shirt with a **G** on it, so all three of them had a **G** on their shirts. They thought this was really funny and started to laugh.

Little Kerry the dog didn't understand what all the excitement was about, but he joined in anyway by scampering about and wagging his tail at everybody.

Then George said, "Look here, do you mind if I call you Gwen? Lady Gwendolyn is a very nice name but it **is** rather a mouthful."

"Oh, I'd love it, really. Nobody has ever called me Gwen before. Please may I try to ride your new bike now?" she said.

They all had a big G on their shirts.

Lady Gwendolyn, or Gwen as she was now called, sat sideways again on the bike. George had to explain that, although it was all right to sit side-saddle on a pony, no-one could ride a bike with both legs on one side.

"You won't be able to reach the pedals like that, so you will have to sit the same way as I do," said George patiently.

He held the bike steady for her whilst she got on.

Once she had settled herself on it properly, it seemed to take only a few wobbly falls before Gwen was riding along the track and calling out that she had never enjoyed herself so much in all her life.

(Well, it's so much easier to ride a bike in a dream, isn't it?).

Gladys and George cheered and called out, **"Brilliant. Well done Gwen. You're doing really well."**

And I expect you can guess what little Kerry said, can't you?

Gwen was riding along the track.

"Woof, woof."

The sleepy dragon woke from her dream to find George and Kerry standing beside her.

George was saying, "Come on Gladys. Wake up. What **were** you dreaming about? You were calling out in your sleep, saying 'Well done Gwen, I've never seen anyone learn to ride a bike so quickly.' What does it all mean?"

Gladys the Dragon closed her eyes again, and gave a little smile.

"Well," she said, "she really was **very** good."

THE END

Gladys closed her eyes and smiled.

TITLES AVAILABLE NOW

1.	Gladys the Dragon and The Lost Lamb	1 871044 65 0
2.	Gladys the Dragon in Gladys Saves the Day	1 871044 66 9
3.	Gladys the Dragon and The Flying Lesson	1 871044 67 7
4.	Gladys the Dragon and The Slippery Slope	1 871044 68 5
5.	Gladys the Dragon meets Lady Gwendolyn	1 871044 69 3
6.	Gladys the Dragon and The Mountain Bike	1 871044 70 7

More titles available Summer 1998

Order copies from your usual bookseller